Barnaby McRuff-Ruff

Orchestrated by IlluminateBooks   Illustrations by Cat Mocha

So we rushed to go home
and we went on our way.

We just got a new dog
and he's happy to stay!

We walked in to our house,
in a blink of an eye,

Our new dog got dressed up
in a suit, hat, and tie!

He moved left he moved right,
danced a step called the jig.

Now he stopped and he bowed,
thought my mom, this is big!

Barnaby McRuff-Ruff
is our dog not a boy,

But he thinks he's a kid,
it's so fun, it's a joy!

The dog hopped on the couch
and he crossed his legs up.

"Silly dog," said the mom,
"don't you know, you're a pup?"

Then he took the remote
and he turned on the game.

Said by dad with a smile,
"this here dog sure is tame!"

Now he pulled up a chair
when it came time to eat.

He looked high he looked low
he sat tall in his seat.

Then the pup jumped on up
and he picked up a fork,

And he dished up some meat
and he scarfed down his pork.

He got down from his chair
and he cleared off his plate,

And mom said with a grin,
"oh my gosh, this is great!"

Now the dog needs a drink
so he gets down a cup.

Then he looks in the fridge
for some milk to slurp up.

Barnaby McRuff-Ruff
is our dog not a boy,

But he thinks he's a kid,
it's so fun, it's a joy!

With a leash in his mouth,
as we stood there in shock,

He went out of the door,
took our cat for a walk!

The boy smiled at his mom,
and he winked at his dad.

"This here dog is the best!
He is totally rad!"

When the sun had gone down
it was time to go sleep.

The dog tucked the boy in,
and then helped him count sheep.

Barnaby McRuff-Ruff
is our dog not a boy,

But he thinks he's a kid,
it's so fun, it's a joy!

Featured creative content provider

Who brought Barnaby McRuff-Ruff to life?

CAT MOCHA is a night owl who likes to paint and code into the early morning.

She spends her spare time honing her dabbling abilities and listening to coyotes howl in her backyard.

Original Idea

A rescued dog has had a hard life on the streets but is finally adopted into his forever home. The only problem is that he thinks he's a person! He sits at the table, sleeps in the bed and tries to walk around on his back legs. He's nicknamed the little gentleman and wears a bowtie, given to him by his new family. This book is about his adventures.

Original Illustration

Barnaby McRuff-Ruff in the eyes of other IlluminateBooks illustrators

Like to draw? Do you want your illustrations in a book? Visit IlluminateBooks.com

ILLUMINATEBOOKS

WE'RE MORE CREATIVE TOGETHER

"It takes a village to raise a child." -- African Proverb

"Sticks in a bundle are unbreakable." -- Bondei Proverb

"No task is too big when done together." -- Hawaiian Proverb

These quotes from around the world acknowledge what we all know to be true - that in all our diversity, we're better, stronger and more creative working together than we are alone.

This work is the result of the contributions of writers and illustrators from all over the United States and the world. The creativity of hundreds of people, just like you, go into all publications by IlluminateBooks. People who have an idea for a book, a poem, a piece of art, people who have talent for a turn of phrase, have come together to form something greater than any of them.

Want to be part of the movement? Go to illuminateBooks.com

Made in the USA
Charleston, SC
13 January 2015